For Alex and Udo
—K.L.

Designed by Tony Fejeran . Special thanks to illustrators Janelle Bell-Martin, Seung Kim, David Boelke, Jeff Garstecki, Andy Phillipson, and Scott Tilley

Materials and characters from the movie *Cars.* Copyright © 2012 Disney/Pixar.

Disney/Pixar elements ©Disney/Pixar, not including underlying vehicles owned by third parties; Chevrolet is a trademark of General Motors; FIAT is a trademark of FIAT S.p.A.; Mazda Miata is a registered trademark of Mazda Motor Corporation; Model T is a registered trademark of Ford Motor Company; Porsche is a trademark of Porsche; Volkswagen trademarks, design patents and copyrights are used with the approval of the owner Volkswagen AG; Background inspired by the Cadillac Ranch by Ant Farm (Lord, Michels and Marquez) © 1974.

Printed in the United States of America . First Edition . 10 9 8 7 6 5 4 3 2   .G942-9090-6-12340 ISBN 978-1-4231-3875-4   Visit www.disneybooks.com

SUSTAINABLE FORESTRY INITIATIVE

Certified Sourcing

www.sfiprogram.org
SFI-00993
For Text Only

MATER
and the
EASTER BUGGY

Written by Kirsten Larsen Illustrated by the Disney Storybook Artists

Disney PRESS
New York

Easter was just one day away, and the cars in Radiator Springs were revving up for fun. As Lightning McQueen drove down Main Street, he saw his friends getting ready for the holiday.

Red the fire truck was planting taillight tulip bulbs.

Flo the 1950s show car was showing off her fancy new Easter colors.

Lizzie the Model T was having a spring sale.

Fillmore the van was decorating oilcans for the town's annual Easter can hunt.

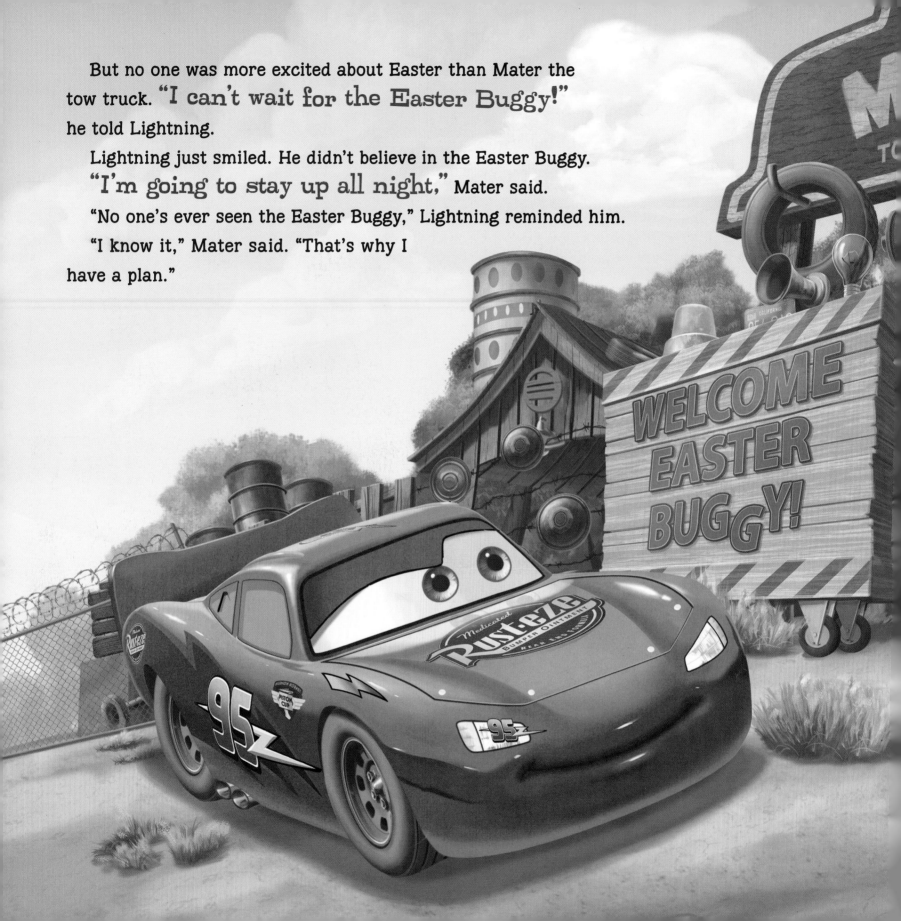

But no one was more excited about Easter than Mater the tow truck. "I can't wait for the Easter Buggy!" he told Lightning.

Lightning just smiled. He didn't believe in the Easter Buggy.

"I'm going to stay up all night," Mater said.

"No one's ever seen the Easter Buggy," Lightning reminded him.

"I know it," Mater said. "That's why I have a plan."

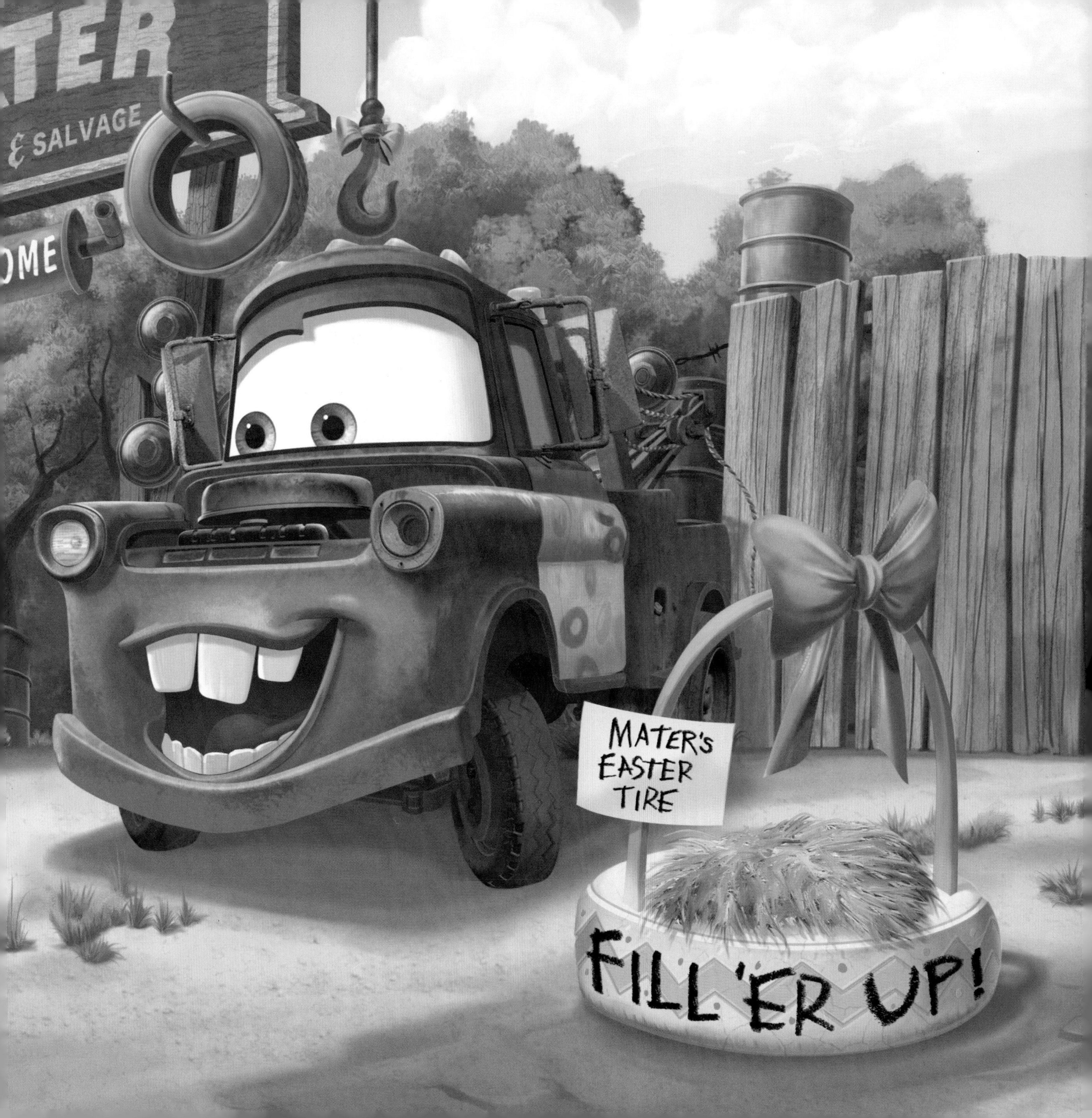
TER
& SALVAGE
OME
MATER'S
EASTER
TIRE
FILL 'ER UP!

Lightning realized his friend was serious. "But what if the Easter Buggy doesn't show up?" he asked.

MATER'S EASTER TIRE

FILL 'ER UP!

"Of course he'll come," Mater said with a laugh. "It's Easter, ain't it? Now, 'scuse me, buddy. I gotta finish gettin' ready. This is gonna be the best Easter ever!"

Lightning knew he had to do something. If the Easter Buggy didn't show, Mater would be so disappointed!

Lightning raced to Fillmore's. "Could I have a few of those Easter cans?" he asked.

"Help yourself, man," said Fillmore.

Next, Lightning stopped at the curio shop. "Lizzie, I need the best springs you've got."

"Anything for you, good-lookin'," said Lizzie.

Then, Lightning went to Flo's café. "I'll take a dozen lug nuts, please," he told Flo. "And throw in a quart of coolant."
"What are you doing with all those treats?" Flo asked Lightning.
"It's just a little Easter surprise," Lightning said.

Last of all, Lightning picked up some headlamps for an Easter Buggy disguise and headed back to Mater's tow yard. "Now I'll just wait until Mater falls asleep," he said.

Lightning hid behind a nearby fence.

He waited . . .

and waited . . .

and waited.

At last, Mater's eyes closed. "Time for action," Lightning said. His plan was to fill his friend's Easter tire. When Mater woke up, he'd think the Easter Buggy had come!

But Lightning didn't look where he was going. Suddenly . . .

HONK! HONK! HONK!

Lightning had rolled over an alarm Mater had set up.

"He's here!" cried Mater, waking up.

"Lightning!" Mater said.
"Did ya see him?"
"See who?" asked Lightning.
"The Easter Buggy!" Mater
exclaimed.

Mater checked his Easter tire. "Nothing yet," he said. "But
he set off the alarm. He must be around here somewhere."

Lightning had to think fast. "I'll bet he's stopping by Luigi's," he said. "Why don't you catch him over there?" "Good thinking, buddy," Mater replied as he sped off toward Luigi's tire shop.

Lightning followed quietly behind. "Good ole Mater." He chuckled to himself. "I should have known he'd set a booby trap for the Easter Buggy."

Mater pulled up in front of Luigi's Casa Della Tires and set down his Easter tire. Lightning hid and waited for Mater to fall asleep again.

Soon he heard Mater's snores. Lightning tried to sneak over to fill Mater's Easter tire. But he bumped into a stack of tires. . . .

CRASH! The tower of tires tumbled down around Lightning and Mater.

"The Easter Buggy's here!" Mater shouted.

"Dadgum!" Mater said to Lightning. "We missed him again. Where do you think he'll go next?"

"Er, what about Ramone's?" Lightning suggested.

"That's it!" cried Mater. "We're hot on his trail now."

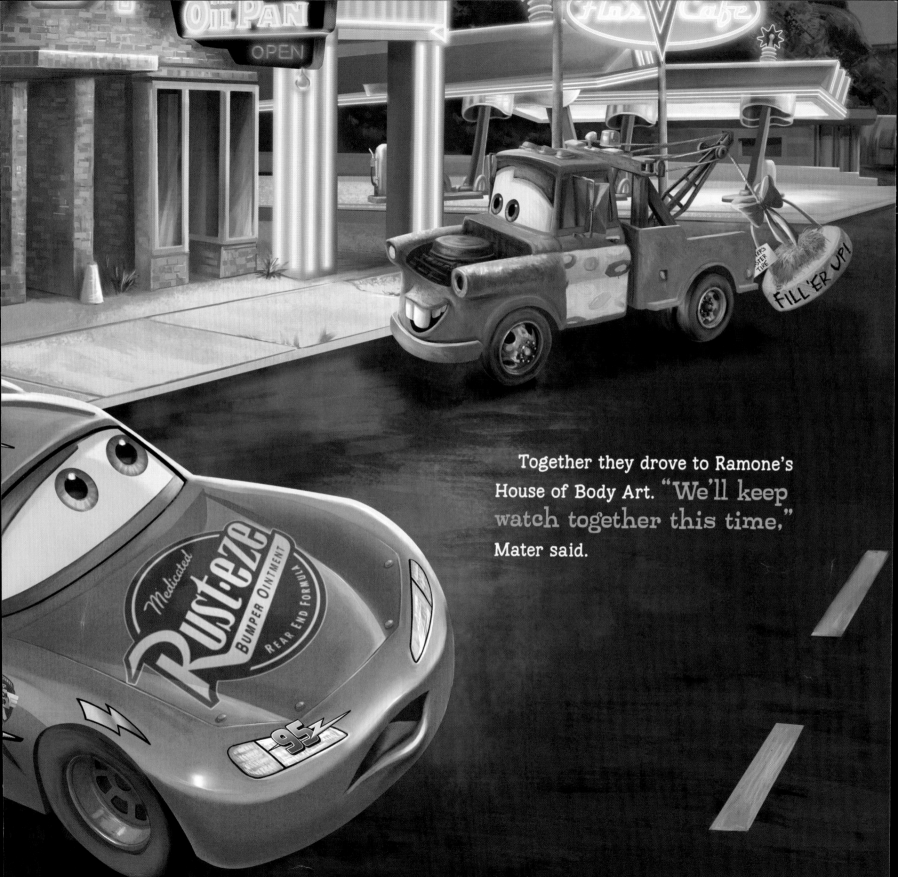

Together they drove to Ramone's House of Body Art. "We'll keep watch together this time," Mater said.

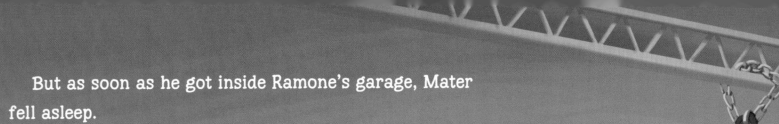

But as soon as he got inside Ramone's garage, Mater fell asleep.

"Now's my chance," Lightning said to himself. He sneaked toward Mater's Easter tire. "No Easter Buggy traps. No tower of tires. Looks like the path is—"

BLAM!

Lightning's back end accidentally hit the shelves filled
with paint. He was covered in bright Easter colors!

"Look at that,"
Mater said, waking up.

"The Easter Buggy
gave you a new paint job!"

"Heyyy, I think I know where to find the Easter Buggy now," Mater told Lightning as they left Ramone's.

"You do?" Lightning asked worriedly.

"Yup, the sun's almost up. He must be on his way out of town!" said Mater.

So Soon?

MATER'S EASTER TIRE

FILL 'ER UP!

So Lightning and Mater drove to the end of the paved road. "We won't miss him this time," Mater said.

As soon as Mater falls asleep again, I'll fill his Easter tire, Lightning thought.

But by then Lightning was very tired. Before long,
he fell asleep . . .

. . . and slept right through the night.

"Wake up, Lightning!" Mater shouted.
"The Easter Buggy was here!"

MATER'S
EASTER
TIRE

FILL 'ER UP!

"Oh, no!" Lightning groaned. He hadn't ever had a chance to fill Mater's Easter tire!

But to Lightning's amazement, Mater's tire was full of treats.

"Look," Mater said. "He gave you a paint job AND a bunch of goodies.

He's the BEST!"

That wasn't all. The Easter Buggy had left
something for every car in Radiator Springs.

"That's a beautiful sight, man," said Fillmore.
"What a great Easter!" Flo agreed.

"I still can't figure out who filled everybody's
Easter tires," Lightning said.

"It was the Easter Buggy," Mater replied. "That's
what I keep tellin' you."

"Well, Mater," said Lightning, "maybe you're right."

"Maybe? I know I'm right!" Mater said.

"Happy Easter, Mater,"
said Lightning.
"Happy Easter, buddy!"
said Mater.